Haunted bathrooms?

Tuesday Herbie met Raymond on the corner as usual. But today he had a book in his hand.

"What are you reading, Ray?"

"Captain Outrageous by Rudy Kippers."

"Is it good?" Herbie asked.

"Never read it. But there are big words in the story. Miss Pinkham will think I'm smart."

Herbie shook his head. "I don't know about that, Raymond."

When they got to school, they met Margie running up the stairs from the girls' bathroom. She looked white as a ghost.

"They're HAUNTED!" she screamed.

"Huh?" Herbie said.

"What is?" Raymond asked.

"THE BATHROOMS!" And then she ran outside.

"Shrewd depictions of childhood concerns and a fine supporting cast of characters make this a pleasure to read." *—Booklist*

PUFFIN BOOKS ABOUT HERBIE JONES

Herbie Jones
Herbie Jones and the Class Gift
Herbie Jones and Hamburger Head
What's the Matter with Herbie Jones?

HERBIE JONES

Suzy Kline

illustrated by Richard Williams

PUFFIN BOOKS

For my husband, Rufus,
who once was in the lowest reading group and who went on to earn
his Ph.D. Thank you for your insights, interest, and sense of humor.
This book is dedicated to you with love.

PUFFIN BOOKS
Published by the Penguin Group
Penguin Putnam Books for Young Readers,
345 Hudson Street, New York, New York 10014, U.S.A.
Penguin Books Ltd, 80 Strand, London WC2R ORL, England
Penguin Books Australia Ltd, Ringwood, Victoria, Australia
Penguin Books Canada Ltd, 10 Alcorn Avenue, Toronto, Ontario, Canada M4V 3B2
Penguin Books (N.Z.) Ltd, 182-190 Wairau Road, Auckland 10, New Zealand

Penguin Books Ltd, Registered Offices: Harmondsworth, Middlesex, England

First published in the United States of America by G. P. Putnam's Sons, 1985
Published by Picture Puffins, 1986
Reissued by Puffin Books,
a division of Penguin Putnam Books for Young Readers, 2002

1 3 5 7 9 10 8 6 4 2

Text copyright © Suzy Kline, 1985
Illustrations copyright © Richard Williams, 1985
All rights reserved

LIBRARY OF CONGRESS CATALOGING-IN-PUBLICATION DATA
Kline, Suzy. Herbie Jones.
Summary: Herbie's experiences in the third grade include finding bones in
the boys' bathroom, wandering away from his class on their field trip,
and being promoted to a higher reading group.
[1. Schools—Fiction.] I. Williams, Richard, ill. II. Title.
PZ7.K6797He 1986 [Fic] 85-43426 ISBN 0-14-032071-7

This edition ISBN 0-698-11939-8

Printed in the United States of America

Contents

1. The Spelling Test   7

2. Annabelle's Party   20

3. Haunted Bathrooms   35

4. The Little Room   46
    Down the Hall

5. Herbie and Raymond   51
    in Paradise

6. Perfume and Posters   61

7. The Murder   76

8. Noontime Showdown   83

1

The Spelling Test

Herbie Jones was an Apple. That was the name of the lowest reading group in Miss Pinkham's third grade class. Herbie hated the name. Margie Sherman suggested it the first week of school. Unfortunately, there were three girls and two boys in the Apples. The girls voted for Apples and the boys, Herbie and his best friend, Raymond, voted for Cobras. Miss Pinkham was pleased the Apples won.

Now it was March, and Herbie's group was still reading in the red book (the one with the suitcase on the cover). His teacher said the stories were about people going places. Herbie didn't think his group was going anywhere.

Part of Herbie's problem was that he didn't care anymore. When he got work sheets and was asked to circle words with a "short a," he circled them all.

"You MUST follow directions, Herbie," Miss Pinkham scolded. Then she would stamp his paper with a monkey that said, YOU CAN DO BET-TER.

But Herbie didn't care.

Monday morning was different, though. Miss Pinkham went to the blackboard and wrote the words:

name_____
address_____
town_____
state_____
zip code_____

"As a special bonus this week in spelling, I have a challenge for you. If you can learn to spell your name, address, town, state and zip code correctly, I will mail you a postcard saying congratulations."

Herbie sat up in class. He never studied his

spelling words, but he liked the idea of a postcard going home. It would be good news for his dad to find in the mail. (Mr. Jones worked the night shift at Northeastern, a company that manufactured airplane seats. If a seat was okay, Mr. Jones stamped "Inspected by #12" on it.) The first thing he did when he got home around 7:00 A.M. was go to bed. The first thing he did when he got up around 2:00 P.M. was look in the mailbox.

"There's nothing but bills," he would say.

Herbie wanted to do something about that.

He looked over at his friend Raymond. He was frowning. Herbie knew why. Raymond lived on Wainwright Crescent.

But Miss Pinkham made it clear that it was a spelling bonus; students didn't have to do it if they didn't want to.

Herbie wanted to.

Usually Mrs. Jones would tack the week's spelling words onto the refrigerator with her magnetic Bermuda onion. "They're right here, Herbie, when you want to study them," she would say.

Herbie never bothered.

This week he carried his list with him wherever

he went. First, he practiced writing them on
paper:

pound sound bound
hound wound found
round mound

Herbie Jones
105 Washington Avenue
Laurel Woods
Connecticut
06793

Then he wrote them in the sand at the park:

W-a-s-h-i-n-g-t-o-n

He wrote them with his index finger in his
mother's meat loaf (before it went into the oven):

A-v-e-n-u-e

In the morning on the way to school he wrote
them on frosty car windows:

L-a-u-r-e-l W-o-o-d-s

At home, Herbie practiced on the dusty coffee table:

C-o-n-n-e-c-t-i-c-u-t

"What ARE you doing?" his sister Olivia asked. She was thirteen years old. Herbie called her Olive and she hated that. To get even, Olivia usually called Herbie "Herb," pronounced "erb," as in the seasoning people put on salad.

"Studying."

"Studying? Since when?"

"Since I got my spelling list. How do you study spelling?"

Olivia sat down on the couch. "You're asking MY advice about something?"

"Well, you do make better grades than I do."

"Herbie, MOST people make better grades than you do." However, Olivia chose to take it as a compliment and so she tried to be helpful.

"Well, Herb" (she was careful *not* to say "erb"), "I write them down . . ."

"Yeah?"

". . . and I say them to myself."

"Yeah."

"And that's about it. No biggie."

"What if you have a tough word like Laurel? I keep getting the a and u mixed up, and I never remember which one comes first. The same thing happens with the o and u in pound."

"Oh!" Olivia stood up as if she was about to begin an important lecture on studying techniques. "In that case you think of something like APES USE RADISHES for the a-u-r in Laurel, and OH UNICORN for the o-u in pound."

Herbie stared at his sister. Then he did a backward flip on the rug, laughing. "APES USE RADISHES! OH UNICORN! Why didn't I think of that? So *THAT'S* how you make it on the Honor Roll!"

"Funny, Erb."

"YOU are, Olive." Herbie continued laughing.

When Friday came, Herbie decided to sacrifice his morning recess so he could study his words one more time. (Usually he played "Gang-Way" with the boys—they would join hands and crash in on the girls' jump-rope game.) This morning he sat in the corner of the playground and wrote one more time in the gravel:

0-6-7-9-3

At 11:00, Miss Pinkham passed out the white lined paper.

"Put your name and date on the first highway," she said. (She always referred to the blue lines as highways.)

Herbie was a step ahead of her. He had it done. He thought about the hours he'd spent studying his words and then he overheard Annabelle Louisa Hodgekiss whisper to Margie Sherman, "I didn't even have to study—these words are a cinch."

Herbie gritted his teeth. What a pain Annabelle could be. And she had the easiest street to spell, too—Fish Street. Annabelle was in the highest reading group, the Wizards. They were two books ahead of Herbie's group. She always used her own pencils instead of the school's. Hers had gold initials on them, A L H.

"Now, boys and girls, the first word is pound.

Spell it please on the third highway. You want to space your words for neatness."

Herbie remembered "OH UNICORN" and wrote p-o-u-n-d. He did that for the rest of the regular spelling words.

"Those of you who want to try for the spelling bonus may do so now—your full name, address, town, state and zip code."

Very carefully, Herbie printed his first and last names. Then he printed his street address. He even double-checked to make sure the "i" was dotted in Washington and that he remembered to capitalize Avenue. When he came to Laurel Woods, Connecticut, he smiled. "APES USE RADISHES," he said to himself, and wrote his town and state correctly.

When he came to his zip code, Herbie was in trouble . . . 0-6-7-9-

He couldn't remember the last number of the zip code.

"Pass your papers in, please," Miss Pinkham ordered.

Herbie panicked.

The children passed in their papers.

"Herbie! You're keeping the entire class."

WHAT was that number? Herbie thought and thought. He thought so hard his brain throbbed.

Miss Pinkham stood before him now with her hands on her hips. "Herbie Jones, if you don't hand me your paper by the time I count to three, you'll be here after school!"

Three! That was it!

Herbie printed 3 at the end of his zip code. "Sorry, Miss Pinkham . . . here's my paper."

Annabelle and Margie giggled.

Then Annabelle raised her hand. "How will we know who got it all correct?" (Annabelle didn't think she could wait a whole weekend to find out about her 100.)

"That person will find a postcard from me in his mailbox tomorrow."

Annabelle beamed. She felt confident.

Herbie crossed his fingers under his desk. He couldn't remember if he'd capitalized Connecticut.

"Will you tell us before three o'clock who will be getting a postcard?" John Greenweed asked. (He was a Wizard like Annabelle.)

"No. And, looking through this mess of papers right now, I wonder if *anyone* will get a hundred. There are SO many careless errors!"

That night Herbie lay in bed thinking about the mailman. He usually came around 1:45, shortly before his dad would wake up. Herbie decided to say a real prayer—the kind where he kneeled down at the foot of his bed and bowed his head.

"Dear God, if it's in your plan (Herbie learned in Sunday School that God had a plan for everyone), I would sure like to be one of those people who get a postcard in the mail tomorrow. I wouldn't ask if I didn't study real hard.

"Bless Mom, Dad and Olive.

"And Me."

Herbie crawled into bed and fell asleep.

Saturday afternoon Herbie sat waiting on the porch. He ate his lunch on the steps, and continued to wait until 1:45 when the mailman was coming down the street. Herbie raced into the house and watched from behind the curtain.

As Herbie crooked his neck to see what the mailman was dropping into the mailbox, he heard his dad's voice. "Guess I better check on the mail."

Herbie sat down casually in the green chair and picked up the book on the coffee table: *Ten Days to Slimmer Thighs*. He flipped through the pages and pretended to be interested.

Mr. Jones, who had just shaved, walked toward the door. Herbie looked up and noticed he still had some soap around his ears.

"Morning, Herbie. Nice to see you reading."

"Morning, Dad."

Herbie waited while Mr. Jones opened the door and gathered the mail in the doorway: telephone company . . . Whistleman's Department Store . . . Occupant . . .

Then there was a brief silence.

"HEY HERBIE! Your teacher said YOU were the ONLY student to get a hundred percent on your spelling bonus!"

Herbie jumped in the air shouting, "YAHOO!"

"That's the best news I've found in the mail in a long time. Come over here, spelling champ!"

Herbie ran into his dad's arms and they hugged like bears.

*   *   *

"So who got the postcard?" Annabelle Louisa Hodgekiss asked Monday morning right after the Pledge of Allegiance. "I forgot to capitalize Connecticut," she said as she looked at her returned paper.

Herbie hadn't told Raymond that he had gotten the postcard; he wanted to surprise him in class.

Miss Pinkham tapped her desk with a pencil. "Will the person who received the one and ONLY postcard please rise?"

Herbie waited a moment and then stood up.

"But he's an Apple!" John Greenweed spoke out.

"Herbie deserves a big round of applause for his achievement," Miss Pinkham said with a beaming smile. "Herbie's paper Friday was outstanding."

Everyone stood up and applauded Herbie. Even Annabelle Louisa Hodgekiss, who was used to being first in just about everything.

On the way home from school, Raymond patted his friend on the back. "You're tough, Herbie Jones. Real tough! Tomorrow I bet you'll be in a new reading group."

"Come on, Raymond. One spelling test doesn't

make THAT much difference." (The thought, though, of not being an Apple anymore sure pleased Herbie.)

"Well, it's a matter of time. A matter of time for BOTH of us, Herbie. I've got my plans too. First I have to buy a new pen, though. See you!"

2

Annabelle's Party

"How do you spell surprise? I forgot. Is there an 's' or a 'z'?"

"You're asking me?" Herbie looked up at his sister.

"Aren't you the great spelling champ at school?"

"Well . . ." Herbie put his comic book down. "Ah . . . surprise?"

"Yes."

Herbie put his hands behind his back and walked back and forth: "You spell it . . . s . . ."

"Go on . . ."

"S-I-R-P-R-I-E-S. There is no 'z' in it," Herbie said confidently.

"Thanks, Erb. You're one in a million."

"Feel free to ask me any word, Olive."

Olivia went into the kitchen where her mother was stocking the cupboard with canned food. "How do you spell surprise, Mom?"

Herbie knew he'd been close.

The phone rang, so Herbie picked it up. "Hello?"

"Double 0 3 0?"

Herbie cupped the phone and whispered, "Yeah . . . just a minute, 992." Herbie moved the phone and phone cord through the dining room and into the pantry off the kitchen. When he closed the door a rack of onions fell on him.

"What's that?" Raymond asked.

"Nothing, 992, just a bunch of onions."

"Huh?"

"Never mind. What's so important that we have to use code language?"

"You're getting an invitation to Annabelle Louisa Hodgekiss's birthday party."

Herbie sat down on two onions. "You've got to be kidding."

"Nope. I was at Mr. D's store and I heard Annabelle tell her mother that she needed nine invitations this year because she wanted to invite you to her birthday."

"Where were you?"

"Behind the magic markers. I wanted to find a purple one. Her mother was mad, too, because she had to buy another package of invitations. They only came eight to a package."

"Man, why do you suppose she wants ME to come?"

"Well, you're the spelling champ and all."

Herbie picked up the two onions he had been sitting on and started juggling them in the air. "I wish people would forget about that. Now I feel like I have to get a hundred every Friday—especially when Dad asks to see my spelling test as soon as I get home."

"That's deadly. Hey, Herbie, I was thinkin', do you suppose Annabelle might use a few of those extra invitations?"

"Maybe."

"If she does, I bet she invites me too. She knows I'm your best friend."

Herbie rolled an onion across the floor. "I don't

know what's so hot about going to Annabelle's dumb birthday party."

"She's a Wizard and the smartest girl in the whole class. All the Wizards will be at her party—except Phillip. Annabelle doesn't like him because he picks his nose."

Herbie laughed, but he questioned Raymond about it. "So what?"

"So they're all the teacher's pets. We go to this party, and, bingo, we'll be teacher's pets too."

Herbie changed the subject. "Why did you buy a purple magic marker?"

"It's for Miss Pinkham."

"Huh?"

"Just a little gift from me. I thought she might like to use it when she corrects papers. Nothing wrong with a little buttering up now and then."

Herbie stood up. "Raymond, she doesn't correct papers with a purple pen, she uses a red one."

"Oh."

"Besides, that stuff goes through the paper onto the other side."

"Well, she can use it to color in grapes and plums."

"I don't think so, Ray, you better think of something else to do with it."

"Yeah, you're probably right. I gotta go now, see ya, Herbie."

The next morning at school the invitation was on top of Herbie's desk. He opened up the yellow envelope. There were bananas on the outside of the card. Inside it said:

COME JOIN THE BUNCH!
• • •

When: Saturday, March 10th
Time: 11:00–2:00 (Lunch)
Where: 322 Fish Street
Who: Annabelle Louisa Hodgekiss
What: Birthday Party

RSVP

At noontime, Raymond nudged Herbie. "Annabelle must have used up all those extras in the second package 'cause both Phillip McDoogle and I got one."

Herbie carried his tray of spaghetti over to a

table. Raymond followed him. "Think you can go?" he asked.

"Probably."

"I'm glad it's for lunch. That means there's gonna be lots of stuff to eat besides cake and ice cream," Raymond said with his mouth full.

Herbie took out his invitation again. "What does RSVP mean?"

Raymond scratched his head. "I'll go ask one of my sixth grade friends. Just a minute."

Herbie watched as Raymond walked over to a table where a lot of older boys were eating and laughing. He didn't realize Ray knew those guys.

Ray sat down again and slurped some milk. "RSVP means remove shoes very promptly. She probably has a very neat house."

Herbie frowned. "They told you that?"

"Well, they said they considered me 'one of the guys'—that's why they told me what it meant."

"Yeah?"

"Yeah."

Raymond took another bite of spaghetti. "What are you going to get Annabelle for a present?"

"My mom usually puts two dollars in a card."

Ray made a sneaky smile. "Maybe you could give Annabelle something of yours that's nice, and then keep the money yourself. You might need it sometime."

Herbie shook his head. The idea wasn't bad, though. He'd have to think about it.

Annabelle's house was around the corner from Herbie's. The big white one with the green-framed windows. A Siamese cat sat on the porch. He didn't look very friendly.

"Hello, Herbie. I'm glad you could come." Mrs. Hodgekiss smiled from ear to ear. She also had a tray of potato chips and some green stuff in a bowl. She said it was guacamole dip. Herbie took off his shoes and went into the living room. He was glad when he saw Raymond sitting on the couch. He went over and sat next to him.

He noticed he and Raymond were the only ones with their shoes off.

"Guess we're the smartest guys here," Ray whispered.

Herbie looked at the bowl of guacamole dip on the coffee table. "What's this?"

"Smashed green stuff with lemon juice. You're supposed to put it on a potato chip. Try one."

Herbie did. It was tasty.

"I can't eat that green stuff myself," Raymond whispered, "it reminds me of you know what," and he pointed to his nose.

Suddenly Herbie changed his mind about the guacamole dip. He couldn't finish it. "Thanks, pal." Herbie looked around for a good hiding place. His napkin. Herbie folded the leftover dip in a napkin and put it on the couch next to him, for a minute.

"Hi, Herbie!" It was Annabelle.

"Happy Birthday," Herbie said. She looked pretty in a pink chiffon dress. It rustled when she moved. And her thick reddish-brown hair was pinned up with two barrettes that had rainbows painted on them.

"This seat taken?"

Before Herbie could say anything, Annabelle sat down next to him.

Squish.

Annabelle looked slightly embarrassed.

"Nice party," Herbie smiled.

Mrs. Hodgekiss came into the room with a poncho on. "Time to eat!"

Everyone stampeded to the dining room.

Herbie followed Annabelle in. She had a small green stain right *there*.

Raymond leaned over and whispered in Herbie's ear, "No one will know who did it. You're safe."

Herbie had to agree.

The table was amazing. Mrs. Hodgekiss had prepared a Mexican theme and there were seven bowls of fixings for tacos: hamburger, shredded cheese, lettuce, tomatoes, olives, hot sauce and diced carrots.

In the center was a sombrero which was turned upside down and used as a vase. Daisies were stuck in the middle of it. On a nearby wall there was even a big poster of a bull and the words *¡Viva Mexico!*

"Dig in, kids!" Mrs. Hodgekiss insisted.

Herbie looked for his place card. Raymond found his next to Margie's. Herbie's was next to Annabelle's. He noticed John Greenweed sat on the other side of Annabelle. A typical girl-boy party, Herbie thought.

In twenty minutes all the bowls were scraped clean, except for the one with carrots in it. John Greenweed bragged about putting the most hot sauce on his taco, but he never finished his. It just sat on his plate. Herbie thought that was funny.

When Mrs. Hodgekiss brought in the gifts, she cleared a space in front of Annabelle for them. "We'll have the cake and ice cream a little later. I bet everyone is just too full."

Most of the kids looked disappointed.

Annabelle opened Margie's gift first. "Oh, it's lovely. Thank you so much. I didn't have any more stationery to write with. Now I do!" She passed the box to Herbie. He took a quick look at the princess and the cat in the bottom corner.

"Nice card, John," Annabelle noted. She unwrapped the present slowly. When she saw the contents she started to giggle. All the girls shrieked! It was a flowered T-shirt and panties.

Mrs. Hodgekiss snapped a picture. You could

tell she loved it, Herbie thought. It was just the kind of present John would give.

Ray's gift was next. "A purple pen . . . how nice . . . thank you, Raymond." Annabelle made a frown in Margie's direction, and then picked another gift from the pile.

For some reason or other, Herbie's gift was the last to be opened. The only thing he told Raymond was that he found something educational in his house to give to her. And that he pocketed the two dollars.

"Gee, it's heavy, Herbie," Annabelle said as she unwrapped the foil. Everyone leaned over to see what the roundish present might be. When the last piece of aluminum foil was unwrapped, Annabelle looked half-dazed. "A can of pink salmon?"

Herbie beamed. "We've been studying Alaska in class. I thought you might like to have some food from there." (Herbie didn't think his mom would miss it. He remembered the can had been on the shelf a long time.)

"Pink salmon?" Annabelle repeated with a sour look.

"Why don't you open up the can? Let's see what's inside." Ray prodded.

"There's a pink salmon in there, Nerd-face," John said flatly.

"Maybe it's alive?" Raymond asked.

"Oh sure, Ray—that salmon is probably swimming around in that can right now." John held the can to his ear. "I hear something . . . it sounds like the ocean."

"That's enough, John. Actually," Annabelle admitted, "I've never seen a pink salmon. Mom, would you get the can opener so we can look at it?"

Mrs. Hodgekiss seemed very uncomfortable with the suggestion. "Now, Dear?"

"Sure. How many people want to see what pink salmon looks like?"

Everyone's hand went up except John Greenweed's.

"Majority rules. Mom, where's the can opener?"

Mrs. Hodgekiss returned shortly and opened up the can reluctantly. "Unusual gift, Herbie," she said with a strained smile.

After it was open, the smell of fish wafted through the dining room. Margie held her nose. John yelled, "YUCK!"

Herbie had forgotten how strong the smell of pink salmon was. It reminded him of cat food.

"Look at all the little black things and tiny bones in it," Annabelle said as she passed the can around.

When it came to Raymond, he turned green. As green as the guacamole dip, Herbie thought.

And then Raymond launched it all over the tablecloth.

"AAAAAUGH!" Margie screamed. "Raymond BARFED!"

Mrs. Hodgekiss ran for some towels. Everyone else ran screeching into the living room, except Herbie, Raymond and John.

"There's yellow barf all over the carrot dish and yellow barf floating in Margie's water glass!" John called out.

Phillip cackled and Margie screamed.

Herbie shook his head. "Are you okay, Ray?" He handed him a napkin.

"I'm fine. Just fine."

"Really?"

"I just do that once in a while when . . ."

"I know what you mean," Herbie interrupted, not really wanting to hear Ray talk about it.

Mrs. Hodgekiss quickly scoured the table with soapy water and muttered some words under her breath. Ten minutes later, when most of the laughter and screaming subsided, Mrs. Hodgekiss called everyone back to the table. "Sometimes these things just happen," she said with a pained smile. "Let's have some birthday cake now."

When all the children saw it, there was a big silence. The cake had yellow icing. And everyone was thinking the same thing.

The only one who finished a piece of birthday cake was Raymond.

3

Haunted Bathrooms

Tuesday Herbie met Raymond on the corner as usual. But today he had a book in his hand.

"What are you reading, Ray?"

"*Captain Outrageous* by Rudy Kippers."

"Is it good?" Herbie asked.

"Never read it. But there are big words in the story. Miss Pinkham will think I'm smart."

Herbie shook his head. "I don't know about that, Raymond."

When they got to school, they met Margie running up the stairs from the girls' bathroom. She looked white as a ghost.

"They're HAUNTED!" she screamed.

"Huh?" Herbie said.

"What is?" Raymond asked.

"THE BATHROOMS!" And then she ran outside.

Herbie and Raymond walked downstairs. They peeked in the boys' bathroom. The smell of Clorox and soap filled the air. Mr. Bob was busy mopping up.

"What happened?" Ray asked.

"The principal just asked me to clean up extra good this morning. He said some kids were passing rumors about the bathrooms being haunted."

"Oh," they replied.

"If there are any ghosts around here, this Lysol and Clorox will get 'em," Mr. Bob smiled.

When Mr. Bob left with his bucket, Herbie and Raymond explored. The four stalls looked clean. There was nothing on the floor.

"Hey, Herb. Come here." Ray was looking into the tall wastepaper basket.

"What did you find?"

Ray looked up at him and screamed, "BONES!"

"Huh?" Herbie peered into the basket. Sure enough, there was a bunch of small bones.

Herbie picked one up.

Raymond raced out of the bathroom screaming and shrieking, "HERBIE FOUND HUMAN BONES!"

Miss Pinkham had a hard time getting the class to be quiet. Everyone was talking about the bathrooms.

"I saw blood on the walls of the girls' bathroom," Margie shouted.

"Really?" John asked.

"Herbie found HUMAN BONES in the boys' bathroom," Ray yelled out.

Before Herbie could say anything, Miss Pinkham loudly clapped her hands three times.

"ENOUGH!" she said firmly. Then she cleared her voice and said softly, "I think, boys and girls, this bathroom business has gotten out of hand. Let's talk about it. One by one. Please raise your hands."

Annabelle raised hers first. "I . . . I . . . saw the word Bl . . . Bl . . . Bl . . . B-L-O-O-D written . . . in blood!"

Herbie raised his hand. "I found bones in the wastepaper basket."

"Do you have them?" Miss Pinkham asked.

"One of them."

Everyone shrieked.

Miss Pinkham clapped her hands again. "May I see it?"

Everyone watched Herbie as he walked up the aisle. Some kids moved away from him as he passed by. Slowly, Herbie pulled something out of his back pocket. "Here."

Miss Pinkham looked at it.

The class turned totally silent.

Margie sneezed.

Everyone jumped, and looked around.

"Why, this is a chicken bone."

The girls and boys sat back in their seats thinking, PHEW!

"Children, I think this has gone entirely too far. *Someone* is playing a practical joke and it's not funny. It's time to carry on with our day."

"I'm not going to the bathroom anymore," Margie blurted out.

"Me neither," John said.

"Not me," Raymond added.

Miss Pinkham stood up and walked over to the

windows. It was beginning to drizzle. "You mean to tell me NO ONE will use the bathrooms anymore?"

It was pin quiet again.

Annabelle raised her hand very slowly. "I . . . I need to," she said, squirming in her seat.

"Of course, Annabelle, you may go. We'll carry on as usual, now that using the bathrooms is no longer a big deal."

Miss Pinkham asked if anyone had something besides "Bathroom News" for the morning conversation. "Is anyone reading a good book?" she asked.

Herbie raised his hand. "I'm on Chapter Five in *Charlotte's Web*. It's good, especially the part where Charlotte rolls a fly in jets of silk."

Miss Pinkham smiled, "You like spiders?"

Herbie nodded.

Raymond cleared his throat and raised his hand. "I just finished *Captain Outrageous* by Rudy Kippers."

Miss Pinkham looked amused.

"You mean *Captains Courageous* by Rudyard Kipling. That's a difficult book for a third grader.

Did you read the whole thing?"

"Twice."

The teacher sat on her desk and crossed her legs. "Maybe you could tell the class what it is about then."

Herbie began to feel uncomfortable. His friend was in for it now.

"Well . . ." Raymond moved around in his chair. ". . . there's this guy named Captain Outrageous and he eats energy pills and flies around and saves ships before they sink."

All the kids were half off their seats listening.

"Just before he saves the ships, he shouts, 'We're here!'"

Miss Pinkham folded her arms. "If you *really* read this book, Raymond, you would have known that *We're Here* was the name of the ship and there were no energy pills mentioned in the whole story."

Raymond squirmed some more in his seat. "Well . . . Miss Pinkham . . . maybe I did miss a thing or two. Us speed readers go through things awful fast."

The teacher drummed her fingers on the desk

top. "Well, Raymond, you speed readers had better slow down a bit."

It was time now, Miss Pinkham said, to start a penmanship lesson. The students were to copy a poem off the board as neatly as possible.

Five minutes later, Herbie walked quietly up to the teacher's desk. (She was recording spelling grades in her little black book.)

"I'm glad you got another one hundred, Herbie," she whispered when she saw him.

"Well, I kind of have a system now about studying spelling," he smiled. "Ah . . . Miss Pinkham, I was wondering . . ."

"Yes, Herbie," she whispered.

"Annabelle's not back yet from downstairs."

Miss Pinkham turned white. "Oh my goodness!" she said ever so softly. "Will you go down and check on her? I *don't* want to bring the subject up again. The class has finally settled down."

"Sure." Herbie walked quietly out of the room. When he got halfway down the hall, he stopped.

Check on Annabelle?

That meant peeking in the girls' bathroom.

He had to do it. Miss Pinkham needed him. If

she asked someone else, everyone would scream and stuff.

Herbie proceeded down the stairs. Slowly.

First he checked to see if anyone was using the boys' bathroom. He saw two kindergarten boys drying their hands. After they left, no one was in the boys' bathroom. Herbie quietly tiptoed across the hall to the girls' bathroom.

"Anna . . . Annabelle?" he called.

No one responded.

"ANNABELLE!" he shouted.

"I'm in here," a soft voice called back.

"Are you okay?"

"I . . . can't move."

"Huh?" Herbie was glad the door on the girls' bathroom was propped open; he could peek in and see if she was okay without actually going in.

"I'm . . . too scared."

Herbie did it. He peeked around the door.

Annabelle was standing at the end of the girls' bathroom in the corner, frozen stiff.

"Just come on out. Miss Pinkham sent me to get you."

"I . . . I can't move. The bathroom ghost will get me!"

"Don't be silly. That's a big joke. Remember those bones? They were chicken bones. Just walk out."

Annabelle didn't move an inch. "It says THE GHOST IS HERE in blood."

Herbie glanced at the side wall. "That's probably red fingernail polish. It looks like the kind my sister uses. Come on out, Annabelle."

When he didn't hear anything, Herbie said firmly, "I'M COMING IN!" (He said it loud like janitors do just in case someone is still in there.) He waited a full minute, then he stormed in, grabbed Annabelle's arm and raced back into the central hallway.

Annabelle breathed much more easily.

"Herbie, weren't you afraid?"

"Of course I was. A boy's not supposed to be in the girls' bathroom."

"But there was scary stuff in there," she added.

"I'm not afraid of fingernail polish or chicken bones."

"You're not?" Annabelle said with awe in her voice.

"Nah, it was nothing." Herbie shrugged.

Annabelle stared at Herbie. She thought his cowlick was kind of cute.

"Let's get going," Herbie said.

Annabelle followed him up the stairs.

4

The Little Room
Down the Hall

Wednesday morning Miss Pinkham called Herbie up to her desk. The rest of the class were copying over stories they had written.

"Herbie, I am going to send you down the hall to see the Reading Supervisor, Mrs. McDermott."

"Where is she?" Herbie wasn't sure what "down the hall" meant.

"In the little room at the very end of the hall. There will be a woman inside wearing a red dress."

Herbie took his time walking down the hall. He wondered what a lady in a red dress would want to see him about. He had a friend once who stuttered and saw a speech lady in a small room. But he didn't stutter. Maybe he was going to have his eyes and ears checked? But then the lady would probably be wearing white.

No, Herbie thought, if it was a Reading Supervisor this definitely had something to do with reading.

When he came to the little room, Mrs. McDermott said hello and asked him to come in and sit down. Herbie did what she said and then folded his hands. He didn't want to get into trouble.

"Your teacher, Miss Pinkham, tells me how well you read orally. You never miss a word."

Herbie put his hands behind his head, and smiled.

"And . . . she tells me how you read books on your own."

Herbie nodded. "Mostly about spiders."

"But . . . these work sheets and workbook pages are something to be concerned about. Eight wrong, nine wrong, five wrong, ten wrong! Goodness! What's happening?"

Herbie shrugged his shoulders, then looked down at the cracks in the wooden floor.

"Can you tell me the sound 'short a' makes?"

Herbie made a sound, but it wasn't a "short a." It was more like a gargling sound.

"'Short o'?"

Herbie rounded his lips and made a sound like a ghost. He knew it wasn't right either.

"How do you say B-L?"

"Like blood, and blue and blizzard."

"That's fine, Herbie."

Mrs. McDermott put a long list of vocabulary words in front of him. "Now, Herbie, I would like to hear you read as many of these words as you can."

Herbie started with the first one—BOOK—and kept going to the bottom word—PERMISSION. He read every one correctly.

"You read nicely, Herbie. Thank you. Maybe these skill sheets just don't interest you." Mrs. McDermott clutched half a dozen papers in her hand. "What do you like to do in Language Arts?"

"Read." Herbie noticed there was a bug crawling toward her open-toed shoe.

"Well, I want to give you a few stories to read and then I'm going to have you answer some questions about them. Okay?"

The bug went into her shoe.

"Okay, Herbie?" Mrs. McDermott repeated.

"Fine."

After 45 minutes of testing, Herbie stood up. "Will I still be in the Apples?"

"Apples?"

"That's the name of my reading group."

"We'll see, Herbie. I'm going to have a conference with your teacher about it."

At lunchtime, Raymond didn't feel like eating his tuna sandwich. It reminded him of pink salmon. "Want it, Herbie?"

"Sure. I hate egg. Here."

The boys switched sandwiches.

Raymond still frowned.

"What's the matter with you?" Herbie asked.

"I'm probably going to be the only boy in the Apples."

Herbie sipped his milk. "Now, Raymond, I just said she gave me a test. I don't know if I passed it or not."

"You did. I know. You read words a lot better than I do."

It was hard for Herbie to say anything. It was simply true what Raymond said.

"We'll BOTH get out of the Apples," Herbie said. "I just know that."

5

Herbie and Raymond in Paradise

"Anything else you want in this lunch?" Mrs. Jones called from the kitchen. She was thankful Herbie didn't go on field trips every day; she simply couldn't afford it.

"HERBIE!" she called again.

Herbie strolled into the kitchen. "I was talking to Gus and Spike in the bathroom."

Mrs. Jones was almost afraid to ask who Gus and Spike were, but she did.

"Spiders."

"Spiders?"

"We have two spiders in the bathroom. Each one has a neat-o web. I've been reading *Charlotte's Web* so I know how much work it is to make one of those things."

"How long have you three been friends?"

"Ever since I brought the book home, I've been noticing corners in ceilings. That's how I found Gus and Spike. Now I know why we don't have flies in our bathroom. Gus and Spike are eating them—sucking their blood and squishing their bodies."

Mrs. Jones smiled. "I'm glad you're enjoying the book, Dear. I remember reading it myself. It was a favorite. Here." She handed him a large paper bag. "There's a can of soda inside too. I would like to give you some spending money, Herbie, but I can't. I just don't have it."

Herbie remembered the two dollars from Annabelle's gift. He still had them. "No problem, Mom, I have a little change I saved over the past month."

"You do?" She was very impressed.

"Sure," Herbie said, feeling a little bit guilty.

"Well, have fun. If you come home from school and I'm a few minutes late, don't worry. I'll be here. I have an interview for a job."

"No kidding, Mom. What kind?"

"Waitress. Our family just can't get by any longer on one paycheck."

"Good luck, Mom." Herbie waved good-bye and ran to the corner to meet Raymond.

Herbie and Raymond were partners for the field trip so they sat together on the bus. It was something they looked forward to for a long time.

"What's an Indian museum?" Raymond asked as the bus took off.

"A place where they keep a bunch of old Indian stuff and never let you touch it," Herbie said, settling back in his bus seat.

"Did you bring money for souvenirs?" Ray asked.

Herbie grinned. "Remember the two dollars for Annabelle's birthday?"

Ray smiled ear-to-ear. He remembered.

"We're rich, Ray."

As the school bus pulled into a parking lot, Ray and Herbie both noticed that Burger Paradise was right next to the Indian Museum.

Miss Pinkham stood at the front of the bus and reviewed the rules she had discussed earlier. "You MUST stay with the class. I don't want anyone running off. We will eat our lunches downstairs in the Reading Room of the Indian Museum. Please remember to put all your papers in the garbage. And be on your best manners. YOU represent Laurel Woods Elementary School."

"What kind of sandwich do you have, Herb?" Ray asked as they were getting off the bus. Herbie checked. "Peanut butter and jelly."

"I've got cream cheese and olive."

"Cream cheese and olive?"

"Yeah, want to trade?"

"Are you kidding?"

As the class entered the museum, Raymond pointed to Burger Paradise. "That's where we should have lunch."

"Sure," Herbie frowned. "Keep dreaming."

A gray-haired lady with tight curls met the class. She was very friendly. She started them on a tour of the museum by showing them a reconstruction of an Iroquois longhouse.

"What's so long about it?" Raymond asked.

The gray-haired lady smiled. "This is just part of what one would look like. Actually there could be as many as ten families living together in one long-house."

John Greenweed stepped in front of the display

and looked inside the skin flap. "Ten families? Man, that must be tough for all those people to live together. I know my dad can't stand my uncle."

The gray-haired lady said, "Uh-huh. Over here we have a fine collection of weights that Indians used to keep their fishing nets in the water."

Margie reached over to touch one.

"Mustn't touch!" the lady said, waggling her finger.

Raymond was glad Herbie warned him about museums.

An hour later, some of the children were dragging. After the sixth person asked Miss Pinkham what time they were going to have lunch, she suggested they go downstairs and eat.

Ray looked at Herbie. "This is our chance. It won't take us long."

Herbie thought about his peanut butter sandwich. "Can you buy souvenirs here, Miss Pinkham?" he asked.

"They don't have them here, Herbie, just postcards. This is a small museum," she replied.

Herbie felt the two dollars in his pocket. His

stomach growled. He pictured a juicy hamburger with melted cheese. It was too tempting.

As the class walked down the stairs to the Reading Room, Herbie and Ray ducked out the door. Since they were at the end of the line, no one noticed.

The boys raced across the lawn and the Burger Paradise parking lot. Only a few people were in line for hamburgers. It was just 11:20 A.M.

Herbie was amazed how well Raymond read the wall chart.

"Cheeseburger, baconburger, chili dog, fries, Coke, milkshake . . ."

"Gee, Ray, you know all the words up there."

Ray grinned. "Easy. What can we get?"

Herbie looked at the prices. Cheeseburgers were 95¢. "Let's order two cheeseburgers."

"Yeah!" Ray shouted.

In two minutes, the boys had their cheeseburgers. "$2.04 please," the young man announced.

Herbie knew he was short four cents. "We have a problem, Ray."

"Not *just* a money problem," someone said

behind him. It was Annabelle.

"ANNABELLE! What are you doing here?" Herbie shouted.

"Looking for you. Miss Pinkham sent *me* this time."

"Huh?" Herbie was very nervous.

"She sent me to the bus. She thought perhaps you had left something there."

"Oh man, we're in BIG trouble." Herbie wiped some perspiration from his forehead.

"$2.04 please," the young man repeated from behind the counter.

Herbie turned and whispered to Raymond, "Do you have four pennies?"

Ray put both of his hands in his side pockets. "Just this," he said, holding up a blue button and a burned-out fuse.

"Great, just great!" Herbie mumbled as he rubbed his hands through his uncombed hair.

The young man who wore a white cap that said WELCOME TO PARADISE was very antsy. "$2.04 PLEASE."

Annabelle stepped in front of Herbie. Carefully

she opened her cowhide purse—the one with her gold initials ALH—and counted out four cents. "Will that do?" she asked.

"Thank you, yes," the young man said.

"Gee, thanks, Annabelle," Herbie added. He noticed how nicely her reddish-brown hair was pinned back with two barrettes. They had little pink pigs painted on them.

"Let's go," Annabelle urged. "Miss Pinkham is concerned about where you are."

The three of them ran back to the bus.

"We could say we forgot our jackets, and we were cold," Ray suggested as he chomped into the juicy Paradise Burger.

"You've got your jacket *on*, dummy," Herbie said.

Annabelle looked up. Miss Pinkham was marching toward the bus.

"Quick, finish your hamburger!" Ray shouted.

Herbie gulped it down in four bites. Ray finished his in three!

"*What* are you doing out here, WITHOUT PERMISSION?"

Herbie remembered that word—permission.

"Getting our jackets?" Ray said with catsup on both corners of his mouth.

"I smell melted cheese," Miss Pinkham stated. "AND hamburgers."

Ray started to shake.

Annabelle tried not to smile.

Herbie cleared his voice. "We're sorry, Miss Pinkham. We never should have gone to Burger Paradise. I'm real sorry."

And Herbie was. He knew he was wrong. He never should have left the class.

Both boys were informed they would be after school for one week:

1. Sweeping the floor
2. Clapping erasers
3. Washing the blackboards
4. Straightening the bookshelves
5. Washing desk tops and
6. Writing I WILL NOT LEAVE THE CLASS DURING A FIELD TRIP 100 times, to be signed by their parents.

Herbie was *very* worried about the parents' part.

6

Perfume and Posters

Besides having to stay after school for a week (with Raymond), Herbie Jones got the spanking of his life. Usually, Mr. Jones spanked four times—the first two and the last strikes were lighthanded. It was the third slap on the rear end that was the killer.

THIS time, all FOUR slaps were killers, according to Herbie. And he *howled*.

"Don't you EVER do a fool thing like that again!" his dad snarled. "Understand?"

Herbie stuttered a y-y-y-y-y-e-e-e-e-e-s-s-s-s.

Then Mr. Jones signed the 100 sentences: I WILL NOT LEAVE THE CLASS DURING A FIELD TRIP.

"Dinner's ready," Mrs. Jones called.

Everyone sat down at the table except Herbie. He stood. He said it hurt too much to sit down.

After the mashed potatoes and green beans were passed around, Mrs. Jones cleared her throat. She had something important to say. "I got a job today."

"You did?" Mr. Jones said in surprise.

"You did?" Olivia and Herbie replied.

"Well, there was so much commotion about Herbie's bad judgment today, I decided to wait for a quieter time to tell everyone."

"Where?" all three asked.

"Dipping Donuts. I'm going to be a waitress there starting tomorrow."

Olivia made a sour face. She knew that restaurant. All the waitresses wore dumb uniforms— purple-and-white-striped dresses with purple caps. The idea of her mother dressing up like that embarrassed her.

"That's wonderful, Dear," Mr. Jones said.

"Wow! Maybe we can finally go to Disney World next summer." Herbie forgot how much his rear end hurt and sat down at the table.

Olivia didn't say anything.

Mrs. Jones noticed. "Don't you have anything to say, Olivia?"

Olivia couldn't hold back the tears. She ran into her room crying.

Mrs. Jones made a deep sigh. "She'll get over it. I don't think any thirteen-year-old daughter likes it at first when her mother goes to work."

"Well, I think it's wonderful," Mr. Jones said. "Maybe I'll even get a fishing pole out of it."

Herbie hardly recognized Raymond a week later when he met him at the corner. His hair was greased down and parted in the middle. He had a white shirt on with a tie, and one crocus stuck in his buttonhole.

"Where are YOU going?"

Ray looked at him calmly. "To school. Where else?"

"Looking like THAT?"

"Listen, Herbie, I think I know how we can get out of the Apples."

Oh, no, Herbie thought, not again.

"All we have to do is charm Miss Pinkham. I am

going to be the perfect angel today in class. And at reading group, she will notice how handsome I am."

Herbie started to laugh. "What's this?" He pointed to the flower in Ray's buttonhole.

"I couldn't find a carnation in the garden—too early—but I got a crocus."

"I didn't know you had a garden at your house."

"We don't. This is from Mrs. Von Whistle's yard."

Herbie shook his head.

"What cologne did you put on? Man, that stuff smells like a woman!" Herbie waved his hand in front of his nose.

"Well, it wasn't easy. When I was looking around at all those bottles in the bathroom, I couldn't figure out which one was for a lady and which one was for a man. So I just played it safe."

"Yeah?" Herbie was almost afraid to hear Ray's answer.

"I used the bottle that had a guy's name on it— Charlie."

"Good thinking, Ray." Herbie still wondered though why Ray's aroma was so sweet.

"Boy, I can't wait to see Miss Pinkham's face when she sees me all spiffied up. I may even move up to the Wizards past the Chargers."

Herbie bopped Ray on the head. "Come on."

When the bell rang, the boys went in the classroom. Raymond sat down immediately and folded his hands. Miss Pinkham noticed him right away.

"I can see Raymond knows how to start the morning."

Ray looked over at Herbie and grinned. It was working already, he thought.

"And . . . how nice you look. Are you going somewhere after school, Raymond?"

"No. Just school." He flashed a toothy smile.

Miss Pinkham smiled back. "Well, it's nice to see young boys dressed up."

Herbie began to think he should have worn his suit—even if the pants were too short. Instead he took out *Charlotte's Web* and finished the last chapter.

"I see Herbie knows how to start the morning too. It's nice to see a student read on his own."

Herbie looked surprised. Raymond gave him a "V for victory" sign with his fingers.

That morning when Miss Pinkham called the reading groups, she asked Herbie to join the Chargers. Everyone started whispering. "Isn't Herbie an Apple anymore?"

Miss Pinkham tried to restore order. "Herbie is going to be reading with the Chargers from now on." Everyone clapped. Even Raymond. He knew it was just a matter of time before he was next.

After lunch, Miss Pinkham sat on her desk. That meant the class was going to have a fun project to do. "Boys and girls, as you know, Mr. D's is a card shop in town. What you may not know is that every April he has a poster contest to welcome spring. Grades 3 to 6 send in their best class poster and Mr. D picks out one winner from the town!"

All the kids clapped.

"Now . . . I think we have *wonderful* artists in our room . . ."

Raymond looked over at Herbie and grinned. Ray was a very fine artist. This was going to be his day to REALLY impress Miss Pinkham. Everyone knew Raymond Martin drew the best Viking ships in the school.

". . . and certainly more than one. So, those

that are not picked will be mounted and displayed in our school hall."

Herbie liked Miss Pinkham. She always tried to make everyone feel special. As he watched her explain the rules for the contest, he thought about Raymond. He had a good chance of winning, but if he did, would he think that Miss Pinkham would take him out of the Apples? Sometimes Raymond confused his thinking on those matters.

The only reason Herbie didn't keep worrying about Raymond was the way the sunlight was hitting Miss Pinkham's hair as she talked. She usually wore it back in a big brown wooden barrette, but today it just fell on her shoulders. He never realized that his teacher was pretty. Her hair, in fact, was as blond as a banana. And most of all, Miss Pinkham had promoted Herbie out of the Apples. She thought he was capable, and THAT made Herbie feel warm inside.

". . . so don't forget to print your name and grade on the BACK of the poster—not the front. And remember the main idea is spring."

When Phillip McDoogle passed out the white art paper, Herbie was still thinking about Miss

Pinkham's banana-colored hair.

Finally, Herbie opened his box of crayons and drew a tree that resembled a big lollipop. He put a sun in the right-hand corner. Just to make it interesting, he put a worm crawling in the grass.

Annabelle leaned over and said as sweetly as she could, "I think it's wonderful." She was hoping Herbie would notice hers.

"You do?" Herbie looked at his poster again. It was probably the worm. She liked the worm.

"Thanks, Annabelle, I'm glad you like it."

An hour later, Miss Pinkham started putting the posters on the chalk tray. Annabelle whispered to Herbie, "Mine is the meadow with all those daisies."

"That's a nice one, Annabelle," Herbie said. Then he looked to see which one might be Raymond's. Of course—there it was—a big Viking ship. It was terrific. It was colorful. The detail was amazing. But Herbie wondered what it had to do with spring. He was suddenly very worried. Miss Pinkham might yell at Ray about it. He raised his hand and asked if he could have a word with Raymond. Usually Miss Pinkham would say you could talk to your friends at noontime, but today she was in a good mood and she told Herbie okay.

Herbie kneeled down next to Raymond's desk. The perfume still smelled strong, but he noticed Raymond had loosened his tie.

"Your ship is great."

"Yeah? You like it? Maybe I'll win."

"Well . . . you've got to make it have something to do with spring, Ray."

"Oh yeah . . . that's right."

Herbie patted his friend on the shoulder.

"You're real smart now that you're a Charger, Herbie."

Herbie returned to his seat feeling like a big shot.

Miss Pinkham handed Raymond his poster back and then added, "I think someone ELSE should come get his too. What do you think, Herbie?"

Herbie's thoughts about how great he was suddenly came to a halt. "Huh?"

"Didn't you hear me when I said to put your name on the BACK of the poster?"

Herbie looked at his. His name was printed in black crayon on the front.

"You'll have to do it over," Miss Pinkham ordered.

Herbie felt like the worm on his poster. How could he EVER think Miss Pinkham was pretty? He hated her now. He took the poster and sat down and started coloring. Her hair was probably DYED blond.

Miss Pinkham gave the class a little more time and then clapped her hands. "Well, class, I think we should begin the judging. Are all the posters in now?" she asked.

Raymond rushed his up to her. "It's a cargo of flowers," he said straightening his tie.

"How interesting, Raymond." She smiled.

"Do I have yours, Herbie?"

Herbie walked up to the chalkboard and set it in the tray. It was upside down. Everyone in the class laughed.

Miss Pinkham walked over and turned his poster right side up. Instead of doing it over, Herbie had just colored over his name.

"What's this?" She pointed to the black scribbling in the lower left-hand corner.

"A dark rain cloud."

"A-hem . . . kind of a *low* one, isn't it?"

Herbie put his elbows on his desk and cupped his face in his hands. "Some are," he said softly.

Miss Pinkham arched her eyebrows—the way she did when she was miffed about something.

"All right," she continued, "now that all the posters are in, we can begin. Remember, do NOT say 'That one is mine.' I want people to vote for the poster they think is best, *not* just for a friend's. Is that clear?"

All the children nodded their heads.

The first one she pointed to was Phillip Mc-Doogle's. He had drawn a house with a rose garden in front. Miss Pinkham asked for a show of hands. John voted for it. Miss Pinkham recorded 1 on top of Phillip's poster.

Miss Pinkham pointed to John's. It looked a lot like Phillip's. Phillip raised his hand. Miss Pinkham put 1 on the blackboard above John's poster.

The next one was Annabelle's. Five hands went up. Herbie thought the daisies looked too perfect. They were all the same size. There wasn't even one bent by the wind, he thought. Miss Pinkham recorded 5 votes. Annabelle beamed and then shot a razzberry at Herbie for not voting for hers.

Herbie was still too angry at Miss Pinkham to care.

When Miss Pinkham came to Herbie's, she cleared her throat. "Who thinks this poster is the best one?"

No one raised a hand.

Herbie was disappointed that his best friend Raymond didn't even vote for it.

Miss Pinkham looked slightly amused and then wrote 0 next to Herbie's poster.

Annabelle giggled with delight.

Raymond's was next. He got 5 votes too. Margie Sherman's got 4. Herbie voted for Margie's. He liked the spring rainstorm with forked lightning. It was neat, he thought. He also wasn't going to vote for Raymond's since Raymond didn't vote for his.

"It looks like we will need a revote between this one and that one." Miss Pinkham held up Raymond's Viking ship and Annabelle's meadow of daisies. She was careful not to say whose they were, but everybody knew.

It was going to be close, Herbie knew that. There was no decision to make here. Naturally he would vote for Raymond's. He wasn't THAT angry with Raymond that he would vote for Annabelle's.

Miss Pinkham took her pointer and pointed to Annabelle's. Annabelle voted for her own. Herbie noticed Raymond voted for Annabelle's. That could be trouble, he thought.

The teacher wrote 15 on the board.

"Those voting for the Viking ship, raise your hand please."

Herbie raised his hand high. He could count the number of hands quicker than Miss Pinkham. It was 14. Raymond lost.

Miss Pinkham recorded 14 and held up Annabelle's as the winning poster.

Everyone applauded except Herbie.

"You *should* have voted for your own, Raymond." Herbie chewed some of his jelly sandwich in the cafeteria.

"You didn't." Raymond peeled his banana, and took a big bite.

"Yeah, well that's different." Herbie was quiet for a minute. "I noticed you didn't vote for mine. Some friend you are."

Raymond answered with a full mouth, "You heard Miss Pinkham, she said not to vote for your friend's."

"Yeah . . . but EVERYBODY did anyway."

"Not me. I want to get on Miss Pinkham's good side."

Herbie had had it. He stood up, holding his lunch in his hands. "I'm tired of your acting hot all the time. I'll tell you one thing, Raymond, you will NEVER get out of the Apples that way. Why don't you start reading a book for a change, instead of acting so DUMB!"

Herbie stomped off and sat next to Phillip and John.

Raymond just lowered his head. Then he took his tie off and put it on the table.

7

The Murder

Herbie walked home alone. As he passed Mrs. Von Whistle's house, he noticed her beautiful garden. When he saw the three rows of crocuses he shook his head. Raymond.

What started out as probably the BEST day this year—his being promoted to the Chargers—turned out to be a LOUSY one. Miss Pinkham jumped all over him for doing one little thing wrong, Raymond thought he was going to be a Charger any day now, and the fact was that Raymond's ideas were getting him into trouble. He looked forward to going home.

When he got inside he heard his sister Olivia running the vacuum cleaner. She was also complaining, "I can't believe how dirty this house is."

Herbie wasn't used to seeing his sister cleaning up.

"What's going on? Someone must be coming over."

"Lance Pellizini is."

"Who?"

"The most popular boy at Laurel Woods Junior High."

"Why would a guy like that want to see you?"

"Get lost, Erb. We're going to study for a test in World History tomorrow."

"Sure." Herbie walked into the bathroom. He had to go. He also wanted to tell Gus and Spike about his rotten day. When he got there he turned white.

"OLIVIA, WHAT DID YOU *DO*?"

Olivia ran into the bathroom. She had never heard her brother shriek like THAT before.

"Geez, Erb. I just cleaned up in here. It was awful—including those two spiderwebs up in the corners of the ceiling."

Herbie screamed, "YOU MURDERER! You murdered Gus and Spike. How could you!" He started pelting her arms with his fists.

"That hurts, you brat!" Olivia slapped him back.

Herbie hit her again. Then he noticed the shampoo bottle was missing its cap. He grabbed it and dumped it on her hair. He knew THAT was what Olivia thought was most important—HER HAIR. He doused it all over with green stuff.

"STOP IT! STOP IT!" She started to cry as the shampoo dripped into her eyes and nose.

"I'll NEVER forgive you, Olive. NEVER! EVER!" Then Herbie ran out of the house and down to Dipping Donuts.

His mother was pouring someone a refill of coffee when he stormed into the restaurant. "She KILLED them!" he yelled.

Everyone in the restaurant stopped eating and drinking and stared at this strange boy who was screaming about murder. One of the customers who was sitting at the counter was a police officer and he stood up immediately to listen to Herbie's story.

Mrs. Jones went around to the back gate so she could get on the other side of the counter to Herbie. He ran into her arms sobbing.

"Mom!"

She held him tight and waited for him to calm down so she could understand him. The policeman took out a notepad and pencil and waited. All the customers leaned over and stared at Herbie and his mother.

The manager, who was busy in the back cutting out donuts, heard the commotion and came running to the front of the restaurant too.

"Tell us your story, young man," the policeman said.

Herbie took a deep breath and then explained. "My sister, Olivia, she killed them with a broom, and soap, and Clorox." He had to catch his breath he was whimpering so.

The customers oohed and aahed as he talked about the murder. The policeman wrote down the words broom, soap and Clorox on his pad.

"She did it because of her friend."

The policeman wrote down motive: Did it for a friend. "Do you know his name?"

Herbie whimpered, "Ye . . . yes . . . Lance Pellizini."

The manager, who was listening all this time,

put his hand up to his forehead. "Lance Pellizini! Lance Pellizini is MY SON!"

The policeman looked shocked.

A few of the customers took a sip of their coffee and a bite of their donuts but they continued catching every word of the conversation.

"I don't believe it! My son!"

Mrs. Jones suddenly understood what this was all about. "Olivia murdered Gus and Spike?" she asked.

Herbie nodded, then he started bawling again.

The policeman wrote down deceased: Gus and Spike.

Mrs. Jones spoke loudly because she wanted everyone in the restaurant to hear. "Gus and Spike are my son's pet spiders."

Mr. Pellizini put his hand over his heart. The customers chuckled to themselves and then went on eating or drinking or smoking or talking or whatever else they were doing before.

The policeman shook his head and ripped out the page. "Easiest murder I solved." Then he put the notepad back in his hip pocket and finished his cup of creamy coffee and his chocolate honey-dipped donut.

Mrs. Jones continued holding Herbie. She knew how important the spiders were to him. "I'm so sorry, Herbie. I should have told Olivia about it. I just didn't expect her to be cleaning up the house."

Mr. Pellizini put his arm around Herbie's shoulders. "You know, when I was about your age I had a pet worm farm. You have to keep the soil moist every day. Well, I went on a two-week camping trip and forgot about them. They dried up like shoestring potatoes."

Herbie didn't think that made him feel any better. Mrs. Jones pointed to a nearby stool.

"Why don't you sit down here at the counter, Herbie, and I'll get you an orangeade."

"Sure," Mr. Pellizini said, "and in five minutes there will be some fresh lemon-filled donuts. Like them?"

Herbie sat down at the counter and shrugged his shoulders. This was the worst day of his life.

When Herbie and his mother went home at five

o'clock, Olivia was still rinsing out the shampoo.

"MOTHER! Do you *know* what Herbie did?"

"All right, Dear, we'll talk about it."

When Olivia found out that Mr. Pellizini was the manager of Dipping Donuts, she suddenly changed her mood.

"You work for him? Lance Pellizini's father?"

Mrs. Jones nodded.

"Oh Mother, I'm thrilled about your job."

Herbie wasn't thrilled about anything. He just went to bed early.

8

Noontime Showdown

Over the weekend, Herbie pretty much just read. He didn't call Raymond or go over to his house.

Monday morning he headed for school. Raymond was waiting for him on the corner. Neither of them said anything to one another until they saw the school building.

"You were right, Herbie. I was being a hot shot."

Herbie looked at Raymond. "Nah, I was just bugged by Miss Pinkham. You know when she bawled me out about my poster . . ."

"There's *no* way I could ever get out of the Apples. I'm stuck for the rest of the year." Raymond rubbed the toe of his shoe in the dirt.

"Wait a minute." Herbie had a sudden inspiration. "I know how you can get out of the Apples."

"How?"

"Just change the name to something else."

Raymond thought about it and then jumped into the air. "YA-HOO!"

After he came back down to earth, he asked, "How?" again.

"Get Margie to go along with you, and her two friends will too."

"Yeah . . ."

"Do you have a name you'd like to have for your reading group?"

Raymond thought and thought. "I don't want to be a piece of fruit again, or something dumb like the Peppermint Patties." (The girls had also liked THAT name besides the Apples in September.)

"I'd like a name of something exciting, different and—for hard workers."

Herbie listened while Raymond thought aloud.

"Maybe Beavers—Nah! Do you have any suggestions, Herbie? I guess I just know what I *don't* want."

Herbie thought for a moment, and then he

said with a lump in his throat, "Spiders?"

"Yes . . . PERFECT! I would *love* to be the Spiders. Gee thanks, Herbie."

"At noontime, Ray, ask Margie to join us. Then be thinking of some good reasons for the name Spiders. Margie is not going to be easy to win over. But, you're tough, right?"

"Right! We're BOTH tough."

When the boys got into the classroom, Raymond asked Herbie if he could borrow his copy of *Charlotte's Web*.

"Sure, it's in my desk."

Herbie never saw Raymond interested in reading a book before.

"Isn't this like the movie on TV?" Ray asked, holding up the book.

"Yeah." Herbie nodded.

"Well, it's about spiders then. I might get some ideas from it. Will you help me with some of the words, Herbie?"

"Sure." Herbie went up to Miss Pinkham and asked her if after he and Raymond finished their morning work they could read *Charlotte's Web* in the Quiet Corner of the room.

"Of course you can. In fact, I don't have much planned for this morning. After the Pledge, you and Raymond can start right away on the book."

"Really?"

"Yes, Herbie." Miss Pinkham smiled warmly. It was rewarding for her to see some interest in reading.

Raymond got the book and joined Herbie at the back table. Herbie helped him with the words he didn't know. After the first page, Raymond looked at Herbie.

"Why don't *you* read it to me and I'll follow along. When we come to something good about spiders, I'll try to learn that part."

Raymond listened attentively as Herbie read to him about Fern and Wilbur and Mr. Zuckerman. He appreciated the way Herbie read—with lots of expression.

On page 31, Charlotte appeared. Raymond waited for the best sentences. They came on pages 37 and 40. Herbie helped Ray with a few words, and after a few practices, Ray got it.

page 37: "Well, I *am* pretty," replied Charlotte. "There's no denying that. Almost all spiders are rather nice-looking."

page 40: "Nobody feeds me. I have to get my own living. I live by my wits. I have to be sharp and clever, lest I go hungry. I have to think things out, catch what I can, take what comes."

Herbie closed the book. They had been reading for nearly an hour. Herbie had to teach Raymond the words: almost, rather, wits, sharp and clever. Miss Pinkham helped the boys with "denying"— neither of them knew that one.

Raymond marked the two pages (37 and 40) with two pieces of paper. He was ready to read the sentences to Margie at noontime. He couldn't wait.

Herbie hoped Ray wouldn't be disappointed.

At 10:30, a messenger came into the room. Miss Pinkham said, "Oh, No!" out loud.

Everyone stopped what they were doing.

Miss Pinkham made the announcement. "Boys and girls, I have some bad news. Annabelle Louisa Hodgekiss has the chicken pox!"

Everybody groaned.

Herbie looked over at Annabelle's empty seat. He had been so busy in the back of the room, he didn't even notice.

"I think it would be nice if each of you made her a card before lunch. Maybe Margie would be nice enough to take them to her after school."

Margie nodded.

Herbie liked to write poems, so he decided to start one for Annabelle. First he drew her in bed with spots all over her face (that was fun, he thought) and a thermometer in her mouth. He forgot that she had reddish hair and colored the person's hair black. Oh well. She wouldn't notice, he figured. He couldn't remember what color eyes she had so he made them black too. Herbie did remember her Siamese cat, so he drew him in next to her feet on the bed.

Halfway through the poem, Herbie was stuck. He couldn't think of something to rhyme with "knows." Hose, sews, flows, bows, toes . . . Yes! And Herbie finished his poem.

When Miss Pinkham asked if anyone would like her to read his card, Herbie raised his hand. She looked at the four misspellings and smiled. "It's from the heart, Herbie, that's what counts. I'll read it to you, Class."

Annabelle, Annabelle,
   sick in bed
Spots on her nose
And spots on her head
Think I will give her a
   brite red rose
Then she nos
   I will tickel her toes
With it.
         your fiend,
            Herbie

All the kids laughed when she finished reading the poem.

"Would you read it again, Miss Pinkham?" Margie asked. "That was fun."

And she reread Herbie's poem. "Herbie is quite a poet."

At noontime Herbie nudged Raymond. "Here she comes, and she's alone. That's great. Ask her."

"Come and j-j-j-join us, Margie," Raymond half-stuttered.

Margie beamed as she set her tray down. "Thanks. I didn't know who I was going to sit next to today. Isn't that awful that Annabelle got the chicken pox?"

"Yeah." Herbie and Raymond answered together (with not too much sorrow).

Raymond thought he would ease into the conversation. "Ever have the chicken pox, Margie?"

"Yes. Last spring. Did you guys?"

Both of them shook their heads.

Margie put a forkful of baked luncheon meat in her mouth. "My mom said it's better to get them when you're young. Want my glazed pineapple ring? I hate it."

"Nah." Herbie said.

"Thanks," Raymond replied, popping it whole into his mouth. "By the way, Margie, I was thinking. Why don't we change our reading group name?"

Margie put her fork down. "Would Miss Pinkham let us?"

"Sure." Herbie interjected. "She told me we could change our names anytime everyone agreed." (It was a white lie, but Herbie thought it was necessary.)

"Well . . . the apple season *is* over," she laughed.

Raymond ha-hahed too, just to butter her up.

"What do you think would be a good name, Ray?"

Here was his opportunity, and a golden one. Ray wanted spiders to sound good so he compared them with something *really* gross.

"I think SPIDERS or . . . BLOODSUCKERS would be terrific."

"AAAAAUUUUGGGH!" Margie sounded. "You're kidding?"

"No, they're good names."

"Well, I'm definitely *not* going to be a Bloodsucker," Margie said as she hit the table with her fist. One of the peach slices bounced out of her tray. The straw in Raymond's milk jumped up about an inch and then settled back.

"Well, how 'bout Spiders then?" Ray said with a calculating smile.

"Ennnnh?" Margie fluttered her hand.

"Of course we're not talking about ordinary spiders."

"We're not?"

"No," Raymond said, "I'm talking about the spiders who are related to someone FAMOUS."

"You are? Like who?" Margie was very interested.

"Charlotte."

"Charlotte?"

"You want that peach slice?" Ray pointed.

"No! It's dirty; it's been on the table."

"I'll take it." Ray leaned across with his fork, stabbed the peach, and popped it in his mouth.

Herbie made a face.

"You know—*Charlotte's Web*," Ray continued as he chewed the peach slice.

"Oh, you mean THAT Charlotte; she was really nice. Mom read me the story and I saw the movie."

Herbie handed Raymond the book. Ray opened it to the marked page. "I happen to have the sentence here that Charlotte said about spiders."

"Really?" Margie got up and sat on the same side of the table as Raymond.

Raymond read the two selections (leaving the sentence out that had "denying" in it).

"Well, I *am* pretty," replied Charlotte. ". . . Almost all spiders are rather nice-looking. . . . Nobody feeds me. I have to get my own living. I live by my wits. I have to be sharp and clever, lest I go hungry. I have to think things out, catch what I can, take what comes."

"Hmmmmm." Margie sipped some more milk.

"What do you think?" Ray leaned on the table, cupping his face in his hands.

"Hmmmm. Spiders are really sharp and clever?"

"Yup," Raymond replied.

"They think things out?"

"Yup," Herbie chimed in.

"They're pretty?"

"Very," Raymond assured her.

"Well, looks aren't everything. What do spiders do?"

Raymond looked desperate. He turned to Herbie. "Important things . . . right, Herb?"

Herbie picked up the book and turned to page

40 again. He remembered something about that.
"Here, listen to this, Margie:

> "And *further*more," said Charlotte, shaking
> one of her legs, "do you realize that if I didn't
> catch bugs and eat them, bugs would increase and
> multiply and get so numerous that they'd
> destroy the earth, wipe out everything?"

Raymond sat back in his chair and grinned.

"So spiders save the world from destruction,"
Herbie summarized. Then he closed the book.

"Well . . ." Margie wiped her mouth with a
napkin and then wadded the paper up into a ball.

Raymond tried to keep himself from getting too
excited. "Yeah . . . yeah?"

Herbie looked at Margie.

Margie continued, "Well, I guess we can call
ourselves Spiders."

Ray stood up. "Super." And he held out his
hand. Margie shook it.

"I'll tell the other two girls that we're changing
our name from Apples to Spiders."

Raymond hopped on his chair. "ALL RIGHT!"
And then he jumped off and slapped Herbie "five"
on the hands.

Miss Pinkham said it was okay with her if the Apples wanted to change their name. She went to the blackboard where the Wizards and Chargers had assignments written in chalk. She erased the word "Apples" and wrote in "Spiders."

Raymond tipped his chair back and sighed. He had done it. The last two months of school were going to be his best.

On the way home from school, Herbie put his arm around Raymond. "We did it! We're no longer Apples."

"It's a *great* feeling," Raymond said.

"This calls for a celebration. Let's go to my house for some day-old Dipping donuts."

"Yeah!"

"When you crunch into those buggers you find out what tough is."

"Like us?" Ray asked.

"Like us," Herbie said.

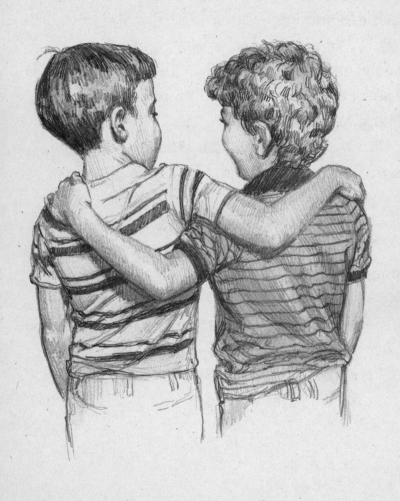